ESP
McGEE
EDWARD PACKARD

EDWARD PACKARD is a graduate of Princeton University and Columbia Law School. He has written eighteen books based on his original and widely copied idea for the Choose Your Own Adventure series, stories in which you, the reader, make decisions that effect plot development and outcome. He conceived of the idea for the ESP McGEE stories while trying to decide whether ESP exists in reality or only in myth. He admits that—like Matt Terrell, the narrator of the series—he is not certain of the answer to that question.

ESP McGEE

EDWARD PACKARD

Illustrated by Larry Ross

AN AVON CAMELOT BOOK

5th grade reading level has been determined by using the Fry Readability Scale.

ESP McGee is an original publication of Avon Books. This work has never before appeared in book form.

AVON BOOKS
A division of
The Hearst Corporation
959 Eighth Avenue
New York, New York 10019

Library of Congress Cataloging in Publication Data

Packard, Edward, 1931–
    ESP McGee.

    (An Avon/Camelot book)
    "5th grade reading level"—T.p. verso.
    Summary: When Matt Terrell, new to the neighborhood, makes friends with ESP McGee, a supposed genius with extrasensory perception, they become involved with terrorists interested in sabotaging a nuclear plant.
    [1. Mystery and detective stories] I. Ross, Larry,
1943–   ill. II. Title. III. Title: E.S.P. McGee.
PZ7.P1245Eab 1983 [Fic]   83-45180
ISBN 0-380-84053-7

First Camelot Printing, August, 1983

For Caroline, Andrea and Wells
with special thanks to

Amy Berkower
Dan Weiss
Marcia Leonard
Ellen Steiber
and
Rosalie Meehan

Chapter One

"**Y**OU'LL love it," Mom said as we stood in front of our car on a hazy summer day and stared at the funny-looking old house.

"It's quaint. Very, very quaint," said my little sister Emily. She pulled at Mom's sleeve. "I want the tower. Matt can have the best room in the house as long as I get the tower."

"Nobody *gets* the tower!" said Dad. "Now let's go in, and you can each pick out a nice bedroom."

Mom and Dad started for the front door—Emily ahead of them—but I just leaned back against our old wagon and took in the scene. The house was kind of neat, though certainly in need of a new coat of paint. It had a big porch with old wooden rocking chairs and a hammock that the previous owner had left behind. The yard was small, but there were some old oaks and maples, and the grass was all thin and silky the way it gets under the shade of big trees. Not much trouble cutting the grass, I thought. The house had two stories and a partially flat roof with a balcony around it. Then, sticking up from the roof was a square room with windows on all sides. That was what Emily meant by the tower, and she was right—it would make a great bedroom.

"Come on, Matt." Dad waved for me to hurry up. I knew he hoped to interest me in all his plans for fixing up the place. His main work as an architect is designing office buildings, but he likes to buy old houses and fix them up. Then, when-ever we move, he can sell them for a lot more than we paid for them. It's a pretty good system, but it means we always have carpenters and electricians and painters traipsing around wherever we live. It also means we move a lot.

"I was just admiring the architecture, Dad. Shall I bring Loser in?"

"No, just bring yourself!"

I took a look back at the car to make sure all the doors were shut so that Loser, our big Newfoundland, wouldn't get out. The windows were open a few inches for air, and of course Loser's nose was sticking out through one of the cracks, as he sniffed all the new smells around his new home—33 Willow Street in Greenport, Connecticut.

"You'll have to wait awhile," I told him. "But don't worry, you're going to *love* this house."

The inside of the house was strange but pleasant. I liked the way there were so many little rooms—like a maze. I took the bedroom at the head of the stairs. It had a slanted ceiling, and from the windows I could see a glimpse of blue through the treetops.

8

"That's Long Island Sound," Mom explained. "In the winter you'll be able to see a lot more of it."

I thought Emily would want the same room I did, but she had already picked out a smaller room facing the backyard. Mom said it was designed to be the maid's room. I looked it over carefully, but there didn't seem to be anything special about it. A couple of days later I found out that in one corner of the ceiling there was a trapdoor that led up into the tower.

We'd hardly put down our suitcases in our new rooms when the moving truck came. While the others started checking off the furniture and the boxes of clothes, books, and records the men carried in, I took Loser for a walk around the block. Then I chained him to the big oak tree in the front yard, where he could sit in the shade and watch everything happening. Poor Loser. Sometimes he'd stand up as if he were going to bark; then, instead, he'd heave a sigh and collapse in the grass, his big tongue hanging out of the side of his mouth as he panted in the midday heat. Mom said he was confused; he couldn't tell whether he was home or whether we were just visiting.

About four o'clock the movers finally left, but we still had plenty of work to do—unpacking boxes and putting everything away. After about an hour of that, everyone was exhausted, and Dad had to leave to do some work at his new office. Mom decided we could take a break. She made a big pitcher of lemonade, and we all sat around under the oak tree and cooled off.

"This place seems pretty decent," said Emily as she stretched out on the grass, using Loser as a big pillow.

"How about you, Matt," said Mom, "how do you like it?"

"Well—"

"Hello there, neighbors!" I was interrupted by a rather

9

shrill voice. Turning around, I saw a short, plump woman striding toward us. She had a cheerful, happy face. In her pudgy arms she held a cardboard box—the kind they give you at the bakery.

Emily nudged me. "It's a cake."

"Hello, I'm Margaret Terrell," said Mom, standing up. "These are my children, Matt and Emily." We both got up, and even Loser struggled to his feet and wagged his tail once or twice.

"My name is Ella Turino," she said, holding out the box. "Welcome to the neighborhood."

Mom reached for the box. At the same time Loser stepped closer to sniff at it.

"Loser!" Emily yelled, and he jerked his head sharply to look at her. Mrs. Turino and Mom both pulled back their hands, and for a few seconds the box floated in midair, supported only by Loser's snout. Then it fell—the cake sliding out and onto the grass in a miserable mound of dark brown goo.

"Oooo! Chocolate layer cake, my favorite!" Emily said, shoving Loser away and scooping the cake, now decorated with grass and twigs, back into the cardboard box. Then she sat back and greedily licked her messy hands. Meanwhile, of course, Mom was trying to apologize to Mrs. Turino—who, I must say, was taking it fairly well.

"Loser, you've got to be more careful!" I yelled. I was trying to act mad at Loser to be polite to Mrs. Turino, but I guess I yelled too loud, because Loser jumped back like a frightened rabbit, knocking over the pitcher of lemonade. There was no use saying anything about that.

"I'll get this cake cleaned up and put it on a nice plate," Emily said as she trotted off to the house. Obviously she was

10

going to eat half the cake while pretending to do everyone a big favor.

I decided she might need some help. "Glad to meet you," I called to Mrs. Turino, as I started toward the house.

"Matt, would you make some fresh lemonade for us?" said Mom in that extra nice tone of voice she sometimes uses when there's company around.

I didn't feel like making lemonade. But I knew it would be easier to do that than to have a discussion with Mom about good manners later on. So I mixed up a fresh pitcher, taking time to polish off a little cake while I was at it.

When I returned, Mrs. Turino was talking a mile a minute. ". . . so, as I said, you folks should feel right at home here. It's as nice an area as you'll find anywhere. Some people are worried about the Prout's Neck Nuclear Plant, but they say it's one of the best managed in the country, and of course with the university near by there's a lot going on. In fact, right here in our own neighborhood there's a lot going on—I guess you've already heard about ESP McGee."

I poured Mrs. Turino a glass of lemonade, set the pitcher down, and stretched out on the grass to listen.

"No, we haven't. We don't really know *anyone* yet," Mom replied.

"Well!" said Mrs. Turino, pleased to death that we hadn't spoiled her story. "ESP McGee—Edward Samuel McGee is his real name—lives just a few blocks from here. He's only fourteen years old—are you fourteen yet?" she asked, looking at me.

"Thirteen," I said.

"Well," she went on, "ESP's just fourteen, but he is an absolute genius!"

"Oh, really," Mom offered.

I'd always wondered what it would be like to be a genius.

12

Einstein was a genius, I guess, and Beethoven and Picasso. But could there really be a genius living in our own neighborhood? It didn't seem likely, but I've learned a few things in life, and one of them is this: keep an open mind.

"What is it that makes him a genius?" I asked.

"Well, McGee is not just your ordinary genius," said Mrs. Turino, puffing up like a proud bird. "He makes predictions that come true and solves cases that the police have given up on. That's not just intelligence—nobody could be that smart. The fact is," she paused dramatically, "the fact is, he's got ESP!"

"My, how interesting," said Mom.

"That's right, ESP—extrasensory perception," Mrs. Turino continued. "That boy may be a block and a half away and know we're talking about him right this very minute."

"How do you know he has ESP?" I asked.

"Well," said Mrs. Turino, "I don't know the McGees *that* well. Just a passing acquaintance. The parents are both *very* brilliant. Mr. McGee is a computer wizard, as I hear, and she teaches Marine Biology at the university. They say *half* their house is one great big fish tank!"

I would have liked to hear more about the fish tank, but Mom said, "What about the boy—Edward?"

"Well, I'll tell you," said Mrs. Turino. "When Edward was only six years old he and his parents went to Wyoming. They were having dinner at a guest lodge in the Big Horn Mountains when he suddenly said that there would soon be an earthquake. His parents said, 'Nonsense, dear, eat your carrots,' or something like that, but within half an hour there actually *was* an earthquake. It broke windows and knocked plates off the shelves and burst a water main and cracked roads—and there were two people killed when a bridge collapsed. Fortunately, none of the McGees was injured.

13

"Well, now, can you imagine?" Mrs. Turino didn't seem to stop for breath. "A six-year-old child *knew* there was going to be an earthquake, and not one scientist in the country had predicted it! There was no way Edward could have done it except through ESP."

"My—" Mom started to say.

"And this wasn't just a one-time thing. Since then he's predicted a tornado, solved a jewel theft, and helped the police find a missing child—to name just a *few* things. Why every time I turn around there seems to be another story about him in the paper! That's how he got his nickname, by the way. A reporter for the *Greenport Gazette* added the 'P' to his first two initials in an article about how he found the missing child. E. S. 'P' McGee, you see, because of his psychic powers."

Mrs. Turino stopped talking, and for a few moments we just sat there. Then Mom said, "Well, that's really amazing."

Mrs. Turino seemed satisfied that we'd been such good listeners. "Now I must be running along," she purred, "but I'm *so* glad to have met you!"

"Thanks so much for the cake," said Mom.

"Nice to meet you, ma'am," I said.

As Mrs. Turino hurried off, Mom said, "Come on, we've got a lot more unpacking to do. Don't forget that this is where we live now, and we have to sleep here tonight."

Loser had come to life and had walked around the tree three or four times until his chain was wrapped tight. Now he squealed loudly. I showed him how to turn the other way and unwrap the chain. Of course there was no chance he would remember. What I'd give for a dog with a decent brain—I mean just a decent *dog* brain!

Chapter Two

O VER the next few days we finally got most things un-
packed, and settled into our new home. Mom and Dad
talked on and on about how they were going to fix up the
house. Emily seemed happy because we got more TV chan-
nels than we used to in the old house. And Loser seemed to
like his new bedroom, a little room off the kitchen where we
put the washer and dryer. One thing I didn't like was that, before, we lived out in the country where Loser could run loose,
but now we were too close to the interstate, and everyone
agreed we should keep him on a chain. That meant Emily and
I would have to take him for walks all the time—mostly me.
Mom said it would give me a chance to see the neighborhood.
"Maybe you'll run into ESP McGee," she said.

The truth was, I was very curious to meet McGee. We

had discussed Mrs. Turino's story over the dinner table that first day, and we were all pretty skeptical. I remember Emily saying, "She's just an old newsmonger." (One thing I should tell you about Emily: she collects words the way some kids collect baseball cards.) Anyway, we soon learned that Mrs. Turino hadn't exaggerated. McGee *had* predicted a tornado, solved a jewel theft, and helped the police find a missing child.

Then, only a couple of weeks after we moved in, the *Greenport Gazette* had a front-page story that was pretty exciting.

The *Gazette* said that J. P. Baron, president of the Greenport Bank and Trust Company, had been murdered, and ESP McGee had been called in on the case. The paper printed a statement by Ellen Sims, a registered nurse:

I was walking home from the clinic about 8:00 P.M. on August 18th. It was getting dark, and as I rounded the corner of Elm and Market streets I was shocked to see a man lying on the sidewalk. He was bleeding profusely. I knelt down and ripped open his shirt. He had been stabbed and it was a bad wound. A punctured aorta. I applied pressure to try to stop the bleeding, but he didn't have a chance. All I could do was ask, "Do you know who stabbed you?"

He seemed to look right through me. I turned and saw another man hunched over, almost on top of me. Then the dying man—Mr. Baron—said, "Edward Hyde stabbed me."

The other man knelt down next to me. "Who is Edward Hyde?" he asked. But Mr. Baron was dead.

I looked around. Some people were walking toward us, and I yelled at them to call the police and an ambulance. When the police arrived, the other man said he was Harry Jackson, and that he was a junior officer at Mr. Baron's bank.

16

The *Gazette* said that the police could not locate anyone named Edward Hyde, and that there were no fingerprints on the knife, which they found in a nearby alley.

A few days later the *Gazette* reported that ESP McGee had solved the case! McGee had explained to the police, and to Jackson himself, why he knew that Jackson had done it—even though Baron's dying words were "Edward Hyde stabbed me." To everyone's surprise, Jackson confessed to the crime!

That night we sat around discussing the news story. I pointed out that the paper didn't say whether or not McGee had used ESP in solving the case.

"He certainly didn't have enough facts to go on, so he *must* have used ESP," said Mom.

"I don't think we have enough facts to speculate about McGee," said Dad.

Emily kept knocking a spoon against the palm of her hand. "I think McGee is wrong and that Jackson is really innocent!" She spoke very seriously, as if she'd given this question years of thought.

"Jackson confessed," I said pointedly.

"He might have been coerced," she shot back.

"What do *you* know, Emily?" I wasn't going to say any more till I looked up "coerced" in the dictionary.

That night I resolved to meet ESP McGee. I decided to approach the problem like a detective. I looked up the McGees in the phone book, but they weren't listed. I mentioned this to Mom, and she said they probably had a private number so people wouldn't always be calling them up and asking McGee for a little prediction or something. This got me more curious than ever, but I didn't know what to do next. Fortunately, the following day I ran into Mrs. Turino, and she told me exactly where the McGees lived: 10 Soundview Drive, a modern house set up on a rise and mostly hidden by big spruce trees. She said the McGees were away on a trip but were expected back in a few days. Thank goodness for Mrs. Turino. She knew everything and seemed more than willing to share it with everyone.

After that, whenever I'd take Loser for a walk, we'd always walk past 10 Soundview Drive. Sooner or later the McGees would be back, and I'd get to meet ESP McGee.

A few days later I was walking Loser—not paying much attention—when he suddenly jerked the leash right out of my hand and took off through the bushes. He must have seen a rabbit or something really interesting, because it wasn't Loser's habit to become too excited about anything. Naturally I took off after Loser, yelling at him to come back. I tore through a hedge, through someone's property, and then through some woods and into somebody else's backyard. There I saw three women—about Mom's age—sitting around a rickety-looking table piled high with papers, booklets, bumper stickers, and glasses of iced tea and juice. As I watched in horror, Loser ran under the table. Two of the women tried to hold onto the table to keep it from tipping over, while the third swatted Loser with a pamphlet. "Go home! Get out of here, you brute!" she yelled.

"Is that *your* dog?" The girl calling me from the doorway—and obviously trying to embarrass me in front of her mother—was about my age, tall and slender, with long dark hair. She'd only said about three words, but I felt I already knew all about her. I could tell she was smug and smart. My next thought was: I hope she's not in my class at school.

"Loser! Come here!" I shouted, and to my amazement he actually came, wagging his big tail and looking up at me

18

with his big brown eyes as if I were about to give him dinner. Instead, I quickly grabbed the leash he was dragging around. "Good dog," I said, and I meant it.

"Sorry," I called to the three women, taking care not to look at the girl again.

"You don't have to leave," one of the women called, as I started back toward the woods. "Come over and say hello— after all, we're neighbors. You moved into the Snyders' old house, didn't you?"

I retraced my steps and she said, "I'm Mrs. Ravinsky, and my daughter Nina is just about your age. Nina," she called; then she introduced me to the other women: Mrs. Murdock and one I don't remember.

"We've drawn up a petition to close down the Prout's Neck Nuclear Plant," said Mrs. Ravinsky. "I'll give you a copy to take home. Your family might be interested in joining our movement. What's your name, by the way?"

"Matt Terrell."

"Well, sit down and have some orange juice. Have you and Nina met?"

Nina had walked about halfway toward us from the house. We looked at each other for a moment, and I could tell she didn't want to meet me any more than I wanted to meet her. But sometimes you can't fight destiny. Nina and I ended up sitting on the glider sipping orange juice—*fresh squeezed orange juice*—and the women went back to talking about the nuclear power plant.

That meeting with Nina Ravinsky turned out to be pretty useful, because, just as Mrs. Turino knew everything about the neighborhood, Nina knew everything about the junior high.

I soon found out that Nina and I would be in the same

school and, in fact, in the same class: eighth grade at Stinson Junior High School. What's more, Nina said that ESP McGee would be there, too, but a grade ahead of us.

"Gosh," I said, "I thought he would be going to a special school for geniuses or even to the university."

"That's old-fashioned thinking," said Nina. "People nowadays know that gifted children should be with their peers in a normal school environment; otherwise they'll grow up to be misfits."

Nina said this with great conviction, and I got the feeling she might have memorized it. Maybe she wanted me to think she was one of those "gifted" children who went to regular schools.

I said, "Oh."

Nina said, "Is that all you can say—just *'Oh'?*"

I said, "What else should I say?"

"Well," said Nina, tilting her head a little to the side and flickering her eyelids at me, "I was hoping you might say something interesting."

I sat there a moment trying to think of something interesting, but Nina didn't wait for a reply. "Of course being in the same school with Edward McGee isn't that big a deal," she said. "He doesn't *really* have ESP; he's just a smart detective."

"What do you mean he doesn't have ESP?" I said, as if I'd already proven it.

"*All* his solutions can be explained by sheer logic," she said, sounding more know-it-all than ever. "He doesn't have ESP because nobody does—because it doesn't exist!"

"What about the Baron murder case?" I asked. "Did you read about that in the *Greenport Gazette?*"

"*Anyone* could have solved that case," Nina replied in a

20

flash. "Baron called out 'Edward Hyde' as a code name for Jackson. That was Baron's way of saying Jackson did it."

I was thinking over Nina's explanation when Mrs. Ravinsky shrieked as if *she'd* been stabbed.

Loser had one of his rear legs uplifted and was watering Mrs. Ravinsky's rosebushes. A second later he was running toward me with Mrs. Ravinsky hot on his trail. One thing I have to say for Loser: he knows when he's been bad. He should; he's certainly had plenty of experience.

"Please, take your dog home," said Mrs. Ravinsky, trying hard to control her temper and be polite. "Please come see us again soon, but next time do leave him home."

"Oh thanks, I'm sorry. Yes, ma'am." I grabbed Loser's leash and reined him in tightly and started toward the hole in the hedge.

"Are there any other kids in your family?" Nina called after me.

"Just my little sister."

"Oh, well, bring her next time, too," said Mrs. Ravinsky. She didn't seem mad anymore.

"But leave your dog home," Nina added.

By that time I was through the hedge and glad to be out of sight. Loser ran ahead, tugging on his leash. He'd had a great time, as usual, and was eager to get home for supper.

As we trotted along, I thought about ESP McGee. I couldn't say I was convinced by what Nina had said, but I certainly was more curious than ever about McGee.

Chapter
Three

THE next morning I took a bike ride around the neighborhood, making sure I passed Soundview Drive. I figured that if the McGees were back from their trip, their car would be in the drive. The top of the driveway was hidden from the road, so I hid my bike in a clump of brush and walked up the hill through the spruce trees to get a good look at the house. All the while I wondered whether McGee might be using his ESP to tell I was spying on their property.

There was a green Volvo wagon in the drive, and I could hear music coming from the screened-in porch on the other side of the house. Certain that the McGees had returned, I retreated back to my bike. Then I took a turn around the block while I tried to get up enough courage to knock on the door. When I came back around again, Edward McGee was in his front yard, only a dozen feet from the road.

He was a lot shorter than I'd thought he'd be. I'd heard he was fourteen, but he really only looked eleven or twelve. He had kind of a baby face and very curly brown hair, and he was wearing large glasses that made him look like an owl. But I didn't get the feeling he would be a pushover. There was something about him that told me he was self-confident. Maybe it was the way he walked. He seemed to move as smoothly as a cat. Watching him made me think of Indians who could glide through the forest without a sound.

McGee didn't seem to hear or see me. He stopped and looked up into the branches of a tree. My eyes followed his until I spotted a furry gray cat, sitting at the base of a limb, staring down at us with wide, blinking eyes.

"Matt Terrell," said McGee without turning around to see who I was.

"How did you know my name?" I asked. Even as I spoke, I felt sure of the answer—McGee had used his ESP!

But he surprised me, as he would so often in the future. "Mrs. Turino told me that she called on your family," he said, finally turning to see who he was talking to. "And I guess she told you that my name is Edward McGee."

"ESP McGee," I boldly corrected him.

"If you like," he said, turning back to the cat.

"Trying to get your cat down? We've got a ladder I could bring over."

McGee smiled. "Thanks. Actually, I'm not trying to get him down. I'm trying to get him to stay *up*. Harvey is ornery. He's always climbing trees and refusing to come down. When we let him out, he wants to come in; when we want him in, he wants to go out. I've decided the only way to keep him from

23

staying up in trees is to get him to think he *has* to stay there."

McGee looked as if he were concentrating. *"Stay,* Harvey," he said firmly.

Suddenly the cat raced down the tree and ran between us. We both laughed, and I guess it was from that moment on that we were friends.

"Well, we got the cat down. Would you like to come in and have some ice cream?" McGee asked.

"Sure, thanks." I answered in a casual tone, but I was excited at the idea of seeing the inside of the mysterious McGee home. As McGee led me through the front door, Harvey scampered between my legs and into the house.

Once inside, it seemed as if we were still outside! The living room had a slate floor and was exposed to a huge skylight. There were three good-sized trees growing right inside the house, and large paintings and tapestries covered the walls. In the middle of the room was a fountain that flowed out of a sculpture of smoothly curved rocks piled on top of each other. You could tell that the McGees were unusual people—and pretty rich, too.

We walked into the kitchen, and McGee opened a big freezer. He pushed aside what looked like the head of a shark! *"Isunus Glaucus,"* he said, as he pulled out a half-gallon container of Breyer's ice cream. "Blue shark. Mother's always running out of room for her specimens in the lab's freezer." McGee scooped a generous amount of ice cream into a bowl and handed it to me, then put the rest back in the fridge. "It's not generally known," he said, "but this is the best peach ice cream on the market, though it's not in a class with my Aunt Nan's homemade."

"Aren't you having any?" I asked.

"Well, maybe I'll have just a bit," he answered. Then he

got the container out again and scooped out about twice as much for himself as he had for me. That was my first clue that ESP McGee had weaknesses just like everyone else. It was kind of a letdown. On the other hand, I was relieved; it meant that McGee and I could meet on equal terms, that we could probably be friends. I didn't say anything about his eating so much ice cream, and I guess he appreciated that, because he offered to show me around.

"Father and Mother are up in Boston for a couple of days. They have to travel a lot," he said, as he led me along a hallway to the other wing of the house.

I hardly heard what he said because I was so fascinated by what I saw. The walls on both sides of the hallway were now glass. Behind the glass on each side were fish tanks—not just tanks but whole *rooms* filled with sand, coral, water, and myriads of fish—some with beautiful markings, others with fantastic shapes like creatures from another planet.

"Mother is a marine biologist," McGee explained. "These aren't here just for decoration—each one is part of a particular experiment."

As we walked back toward the front hall, we passed a smaller aquarium. There was only one fish in it, but it was an especially beautiful one with brilliant yellow, green, and blue stripes. I noticed that Harvey had jumped onto a table at the end of the hall. He sat there, absolutely motionless, watching the beautiful fish.

"I don't know how he'll do it," said McGee, "but I have a feeling that some day, Harvey's going to get that fish." Then he led me into a library with bookshelves up to the ceiling.

"What does your Dad do?" I asked.

"Oh, he's an AI expert," McGee replied.

"AI—what's that?"

"Artificial Intelligence. He tries to design computers that can think as well as human beings."

"Gosh, has he had much success?"

"Listen." McGee flicked a switch on a console, adjusted a few dials, and music filled the room. It sounded like a flute only with a richer tone, almost like an organ. I listened, hypnotized by the melody, until McGee abruptly shut it off. "That music was composed by one of Dad's computers and played on a computer-controlled instrument designed by another computer. Dad's computers can also design factories and even write poetry, though it's not very good poetry."

With parents like that, I thought, how could McGee be anything but a genius? Then we went up to his room, and I was relieved to see that it was like any other kid's, except there were a lot more books scattered all over the place. Many of them seemed to be about psychology and mysticism. A big old book with yellowed pages lay open on the floor. I glanced at the title—*Secrets of the Great Mystics*—and I wanted to ask McGee what the book contained. Another was titled *Ad-*

vanced Probability Theory and another *Logic and Fallacy.* If McGee could understand these books, what did he need to go to school for?

"You can read those later if you want," he said. "Here's what I really want to show you." He opened a closet door; behind it was utter blackness. I couldn't understand why no light seemed to get into that closet. Then he flicked a switch and suddenly a tiger stood before us—its green eyes glaring, its huge teeth ready to tear us to shreds.

I let out a yell.

"A hologram," McGee said as he flipped the switch and extinguished the extraordinary image.

I guess I must have looked a little shaken up because he asked if I was okay.

"Yeah," I said, trying to sound relaxed again, "but it's incredible. What *is* a hologram?"

McGee took a deep breath. "According to my father, it's a recording of patterns of laser light waves reflected from an object onto the emulsion of light-sensitive film, resulting in a three-dimensional image focused in space."

"That's interesting," I said with a straight face. "But how does it actually work?"

"The fact is," said McGee, "I really don't understand it myself."

I smiled and said, "I don't have anything like that to show you, but since your parents are away this evening, how would you like to come over to our house for dinner? I know Mom and Dad would like to meet you."

"Sounds great," said McGee. "Let me check with Father."

"Can you reach him by phone?"

"I don't need to." McGee smiled. "My parents are away a

28

lot, so Father programmed the computer to communicate with me. Follow me."

McGee led me downstairs to a special computer room connected to Mr. McGee's study. He flicked a couple of switches on one of the computers; a large TV screen lit up, and the image of a thin, gray-haired man appeared. "Hello, Edward, how are things going?"

"Fine, Father. I'm checking in because my new friend Matt Terrell is here with me. His family moved in on Willow Street a few weeks ago, and I wanted to let you know I'd be over there for dinner this evening. Okay?"

"Sure, son, if it's okay with your mother. Anything else?"

"Yeah," McGee said. "I've been having trouble programming the environmental warning system for the habitat tank."

"That's a tricky system," the computer—that is, McGee's Dad—said. "The fail-safe will hold things till I get back; then we'll work on it together."

"Okay. Talk to you later, Father," said McGee. He looked at me briefly. "Now I'll just check with Mother." He flicked another switch and instantly a pretty, dark-haired woman appeared on the screen. McGee looked a lot like her.

"Hi, Mother," said McGee. "Just checking to let you know I'll be over at my friend Matt Terrell's for dinner, okay?"

"Okay," Mrs. McGee said, "if you've written your grandparents, as you promised."

"I'll write them tomorrow," McGee said.

"No, you've been promising to write them 'tomorrow' for over a week. Now it's time to actually do it. You've not been very thoughtful, Edward."

"I *have* been thoughtful," McGee replied. "I've thought about them every day, and I'll write them tomorrow, definitely."

"Edward . . ." his mother said in an exasperated tone of voice, but she didn't get to finish her sentence; McGee flipped the switch, and her image disappeared from the screen.

"Gosh," I said, "doesn't your mother mind if you turn her off like that in the middle of a sentence?"

"I had no choice," McGee said. "I watched Dad write the *'Edward you promised'* program. That argument would have gone on for half an hour, and I would have lost it anyway. Sorry, Matt, but I can't come over to your house. I've got to write my grandparents tonight. And, as a matter of fact, I just remembered that I've got a class starting in about twenty minutes, so I've got to get out of here."

School hadn't even started yet, and McGee was already going to a class. "You're not *teaching* this class, are you?"

"Not even close. I'm just a beginner." McGee led me to the front hall, where he picked up a small knapsack lying on a chair. "I'm taking T'ai-chi."

I must have looked blank because McGee began explaining.

"T'ai-chi is a Chinese system of movements that teaches you how to relax your body and concentrate your inner strength. It's supposed to make you healthier, and if you get really good at it, it's an incredible martial art."

"You mean like kung fu or karate?"

"They're all related, but T'ai-chi's different. You don't learn to punch or kick. You can't use it to fight at first. But the masters are unbeatable. Their energy and awareness are so concentrated that an attacker can't even land a blow. I've seen them—it's as if they've got a force field around them, as if they've developed a sixth sense."

My head was whirling with everything I'd seen and heard in McGee's house, but I had to ask him one question: "Tell
30

me, McGee, how did you get Harry Jackson to confess to the Baron murder?"

"The solution was obvious," McGee said. "All you have to do is read *Dr. Jekyll and Mr. Hyde* by Robert Louis Stevenson. Edward Hyde and Henry Jekyll are the same person. Jekyll is a good man, but sometimes he's overcome by a violent criminal urge. Then he turns—mentally—into a monster named Edward Hyde."

"But why didn't Baron just say it was Jackson who had stabbed him?" I asked. "Why did he say it was Edward Hyde?"

McGee smiled. "Because at that moment Jackson was standing right over poor Ellen Sims. Baron knew that if he accused Jackson, Jackson would almost certainly kill her to silence her. Edward Hyde was a code name for Jackson that Baron thought he could use without endangering Ellen Sims.

He took a chance—a dangerous chance—that Jackson didn't know the story of Edward Hyde. When I confronted Jackson with this he quickly broke down and confessed. He was in a very shaky mental state."

So Nina was right, I thought. "Edward Hyde" *was* a code for Jackson. "It seems you used logic more than ESP to solve this one," I said.

"I would say so, too," McGee replied, "but I wonder why I decided to read *Dr. Jekyll and Mr. Hyde* the same day Baron was murdered."

McGee saw me to the front door, and I thanked him for showing me around his fabulous house and introducing me to his parents—or as much of his parents as had been programmed into the computer.

As I biked home my head was spinning. I never imagined I'd meet anyone like McGee or see a house like his. Still, I couldn't help but wonder how happy he could be only being able to talk to his parents on the computer so much of the time. No matter how good the computer was, it couldn't *always* say exactly what McGee's parents would. Wouldn't he miss having the real thing?

Chapter
Four

MOM and Dad wanted to hear all the details of my visit to the McGee house.

"Well," said Mom when I finished, "you must ask Edward over again. He sounds like a very nice boy."

"I want to go see the fish," Emily said.

Dad, of course, was most interested in the architecture and how the house was built. "It must have special steel members to support the weight of those aquariums, unless they rest on bedrock," he said.

"I want to see the fish," Emily repeated.

"It's kind of hard to ask him over here," I said. "This house would probably seem pretty dull to him."

"If he's a nice person it won't matter to him whether your house is plain or fancy," said Mom. "People and friendship are more important than status symbols like aquariums and computers."

"They're not status symbols," Dad put in. "They're part of the McGees' work."

"His house doesn't have a tower," Emily observed.

After that the conversation drifted into general confusion, as it often does around our house. But dinner tasted very good. No computer could learn to cook like Mom.

The next morning I sat around thinking about calling up ESP McGee, but first of all I wanted to think of something interesting for us to do. I had just decided to ask him if he wanted to bike down to the pier to go fishing when the phone rang. It was McGee himself!

"I knew you were about to call me," he said.

"You really *do* have ESP!" I replied, thinking that he would admit it. Instead he just said, "Not necessarily . . ."

I didn't get a chance to follow up on that, because McGee went on to ask me if I'd like to bike out to his aunt and uncle's farm. "It's about four miles out of town, and there are a lot of hills to climb, but I think you'll find it an interesting trip. Besides, Aunt Nan makes the best homemade ice cream you'll ever taste."

"Sure, I'm ready any time," I said, hoping I wouldn't have any trouble getting Mom to okay the trip.

"I think it's a beautiful day for a bike trip," she said when I asked. "Just bring some juice or water along. You'll need it after climbing those hills!"

"Mom says you're going to a farm," Emily said, as I started out the door.

"Uh-huh."

"Well, if it's a dairy farm, you'd better watch out for

34

bulls," she said. "Some of them will charge at the slightest provocation."

"Provocation" was obviously Emily's new word for the day. I suppose all little sisters have something obnoxious about them.

It took McGee and me most of the morning to get out to the farm. It was hilly, all right, and there were a lot more up hills than down hills. But it was a fairly cool day, and it was nice to be in the country and get a workout. Aside from helping Mom set up the house, doing a little fishing, and going to the beach, I'd been sitting around a lot. Knowing someone in the neighborhood made a difference.

McGee's aunt and uncle's farm wasn't really big—just about a dozen beef cattle, some Holsteins, a couple of horses, a greenhouse, and a vegetable garden. His Aunt Nan was the only one there. His uncle had gone to the lumberyard and wasn't due back until after lunch. She was real pleasant and said she'd have some lunch for us in about an hour. "And the ice cream isn't ready yet," she said to McGee, making me wonder if she had a little ESP herself, since he hadn't asked for any.

"Come on out to the barn," McGee said. "I want you to meet Flora."

I followed along and watched while McGee led an old grayish mare out of her stall. The horse didn't look as if she would be much good for riding, but she seemed obedient and good tempered, and, since I don't ride or know much about horses, I was glad of that. But I decided that if McGee wanted me to climb up on that horse, I'd just say forget it.

"This is Flora," McGee explained as he slipped a sugar lump to her, "and, believe it or not, she has ESP."

Well this surprised me. McGee wouldn't even admit that *he* had ESP, but here he was claiming that a horse did.

"Watch," said McGee, and you can believe I watched.

He pulled a deck of cards out of his back pocket. "Now," he said, "Flora will stamp her hoof if the card I turn up is a face card." McGee shuffled the deck, cut it, and shuffled it again while Flora looked on. She didn't seem too interested, and it certainly didn't look as if her ESP was working. Finally, McGee picked out a card and held it up so that Flora could only see the back but we could see the face. It was the three of clubs. "Well, Flora?" he said. Nothing happened. McGee picked out one card after another: the three of diamonds, the ten of clubs, the six of spades. Each time he showed the card to me and put the same question to the horse. Still nothing happened. Then he pulled out the Queen of Hearts. "Well, Flora?" he said, and this time Flora stamped her hoof. McGee repeated the process several times. Flora never missed a face card.

I looked around, but there were no mirrors. There was no way Flora could see those cards.

"Are you *sure* there isn't some trick to this?" I asked.

McGee smiled. "Well, if it is a trick, it produces the same effect as ESP. Which would you rather believe in?"

Before I could figure that one out, McGee suggested we climb to the north field, which was the highest part of the land.

"There used to be an old church up here," he said. "There was even a small cemetery over in the lower pasture. Aunt Nan claims it's haunted. I've never seen a ghost or anything, but it feels different down there." McGee pointed to a pasture where a handsome red bull was munching away on the grass. "Anyway, Gideon doesn't seem to mind."

36

I thought of Emily's warning, but McGee didn't seem to have any intention of provoking the bull. We just sat up on the hill, watching the rest of the herd graze. McGee didn't say a word for about half an hour. I'd never met anyone my age who could stay quiet for so long and make you feel as if you didn't dare interrupt the silence.

After a while a chipmunk came out from a chink in a stone wall, scampered up to McGee, and sniffed at his outstretched hand. McGee kept his eyes on it but didn't move.

"Does he have ESP, too?" I asked softly, thinking a trained horse is one thing, but a trained chipmunk is going too far.

"I'm not sure," McGee answered softly. "I've never met this one before." Whether the chipmunk had ESP or not, he certainly was fascinated by McGee, who began speaking in a low voice, saying nonsense things like, "You come here in June when the cow meets the moon?"

The chipmunk started making little chattering noises right back at him. Then a red ant bit me, I swatted it, and the chipmunk bolted.

McGee sighed. "Matt, you have to be very still around animals."

After that we went back to the barn and McGee showed me his uncle's collection of antique farm tools. Then we went in for lunch with Aunt Nan: hamburgers, and corn and tomatoes right out of the garden, and homemade peach ice cream that has to be the best in the world.

The bike ride back home was great, too, because it was mostly downhill, but the hills weren't so steep that you had to brake. I hate having to brake; I feel as if I'm wasting the gravity that's giving me a good ride.

We were going so fast most of the time that we didn't talk much. I kept thinking about the way the chipmunk had acted around McGee. And about Flora. McGee's card routine with Flora could have been nothing more than a clever magic trick. But that scene with the chipmunk wasn't any trick. It really happened.

Chapter
Five

D^{AD} had time off and our family drove up to the White Mountains in New Hampshire. We went hiking for a week and slept in little cabins up in the mountains. It was fun, especially the last part—climbing through a misty world of weird rocks and tundra up to the summit of Mount Washington. When we got home, the weather turned cool. There was that certain feel to the air and a weakening of the sun. Summer was over.

Two days later I walked through the front door of Stinson Junior High School. To tell the truth, I had a kind of queasy feeling in my stomach. I don't like starting a new school—meeting all the kids and teachers, finding out where everything is, trying to act cool and relaxed. I hate it actually, but I keep thinking that in a couple of weeks I'll get used to it, and I'll know my way around, and I'll have made some friends. So I just go through with it, and if you saw me you'd see that I smile a lot. One reason is that I assume everybody is a decent person.

"You new here? You look a little lost." Spotted as a new kid the moment I walked in by a boy with a ruddy face and frizzy blond hair.

"Yeah," I said. "I'm Matt Terrell."

"Jack Hopper. What grade are you in?"

"Eighth."

"Me, too. All eighth graders are supposed to sign in at the office. I'll show you where it is."

I followed Jack down the corridor, looking around to size up the other kids. "Here's the office," he said and opened the door. I was sort of not thinking and I took a couple of steps inside before I realized it was just a room filled with school equipment—mops and buckets and extra blackboards, amplifiers and broken gym equipment. The door swung shut behind me, but it didn't lock and I was out of there in a flash.

"Just kidding," said Jack. "No kidding now, you should go down there to the Administration Office and get assigned." He pointed out a door at the end of the hall.

I felt like slugging him, but I said thanks and headed on down to the office. They assigned me to Mrs. Bradshaw's class. She was tall and had dark hair with thick gray streaks over her ears, as if all her gray hairs had grown in just those places. I wondered how that happened. Mrs. Bradshaw said she was glad she would be my advisor and English teacher and that there were several "transferees" this year and she thought I'd like the kids here a lot and would I take a seat now because class was going to begin. Then I practically bumped into Nina Ravinsky.

41

"Hello," I said.

She stared at me and said, "Why hello there—and how is your cute little dog?"

Some people never let you forget. I just walked past her down the aisle and took a desk in the back of the room.

What I'd seen of the kids so far wasn't too encouraging, but Mrs. Bradshaw seemed pretty nice, although I could tell right away that she wasn't the kind who tolerated any fooling around. She knew how to keep the class in order, but she could smile, too, and that makes a difference.

All the kids had to stand up and say their names and introduce themselves to the transferees (that was me and a couple of others who'd moved to Greenport over the summer). Of course, we had to introduce ourselves, too; then we all had to tell a little about what we'd done over the summer and what our interests and hobbies were.

Jack Hopper, the kid who'd showed me into the maintenance room, was in the class. He started out by saying that over the summer he had learned that he was really an alien life form. That produced a real test of Mrs. Bradshaw's skill at quieting a noisy class in a hurry, and she did it with just the word *"Next."*

One of the kids whose name I remembered from the start was Doug Viladis, a well-built guy with long wavy hair. He said that he had learned to fly a glider while visiting his uncle in Vermont. I thought that was pretty impressive. I hadn't really done anything special, except meet ESP McGee.

Then there was Nora Lindstrom, a tall, pale, beautiful girl. My first thought on seeing her was that I could just sit and look at her all day long. She seemed kind of cold when she talked, but I thought, maybe she's shy because she's so beau-

42

tiful. Another girl I liked was Sue Tuttle. She was short and perky, and she had flashing green eyes and a terrific laugh.

One kid I didn't like was Hank Gruder. He was big, heavy, and looked as if he spent a lot of time lifting weights. He seemed too big and too old to be in eighth grade. I wondered if he'd been left back a couple of times. He didn't look up from his desk while he talked, and all he said was that over the summer he'd put in some heavy time at the Video Arcade, but that his main interest was hunting. Well, there are hunters and there are hunters, and I made a mental note to stay clear of Hank Gruder.

When my turn came, I felt I didn't have much to say. But, to keep from saying nothing, I said I'd gone hiking in the White Mountains and that I was interested in ESP. Several other kids said they were, too, which wasn't so surprising considering ESP McGee was in the same school. Afterward, Mrs. Bradshaw said that there was going to be an ESP Club and that Mr. Maynard, the social studies teacher, was going to be the faculty advisor. Anyone who was interested was to meet with him in Room 105 a week from that Friday, after school let out.

I decided I would certainly join the club. Maybe I'd learn more that way than I would by talking to ESP McGee. He didn't seem very willing to explain things to me; besides, since he was a grade ahead of me, he wouldn't be in any of the same classes and I might not see him that much.

By the time school let out I was tired from trying to remember who everyone was and where all my classes were and what I needed for gym and everything else. As I walked down the steps I saw three guys standing around as if they were waiting for something to happen. One of them was Hank Gruder, and the other two must have been ninth graders or maybe even in high school.

I picked up my pace, but Gruder stepped in front of me. "Say, you're new this year," he said. "I want to help you make the right friends."

I didn't like his tone. "Thanks, I got to get home early."

"You don't seem too friendly," said the biggest of the other two, crowding me. "My name's Phil. What's yours?"

"Matt," I said.

"Matt *Terrell*," Gruder added as Phil shook my hand with a grip that made me wince though I tried not to.

Something told me that sooner or later I'd have to deal with these guys, and that I'd better do it now. My Dad once told me that the best way to handle bullies is not to run and not to meet them head on, but to kind of throw them off guard. "Think of them as rhinoceroses," he said. "If you run, they'll outrun you; if you battle, they'll mow you down. You have to sidestep—not just physically, but mentally."

"Well, I'm glad to meet you," I said, and I whirled around and shook hands with the other guy, giving him a pretty good squeeze myself. "Matt Terrell," I said with a big smile.

"I'm Frank." He grunted out the words and forgot to try to hurt my hand, which I'm sure he would have done if I hadn't grabbed his first.

That little move seemed to change their mood. They seemed a bit more respectful of me, though still cool and tough. I decided to stay awhile and play their game. We had a conversation about the "stupid school" and the "stupid principal," and I was just about to slip away when Gruder asked me if I wanted to join their ESP Club.

44

"I'm going to the meeting next week in Mr. Maynard's room," I said. "Is that the same club as yours?"

"No, no," Gruder said. "This is a club *we're* forming, but you can be in it. We're going to find out about ESP the fast way."

"What way is that?" I asked.

"Well, it's like this." Phil rested his clammy hand on my shoulder. "We're going to grab McGee on his way home from school Friday. Then we'll take him to a special place and make him tell us *everything* he knows."

"You'll be with us, won't you?" Gruder said.

"Sure, sure, I'll let you know tomorrow." I turned and swiftly walked away without looking back. I thought they might come after me and jump me from behind, but they didn't.

Chapter
Six

YOU can bet that when I got home I phoned McGee to warn him about what he could expect from Gruder and his friends Friday afternoon.

He thanked me for passing along the information and said he wasn't at all surprised to hear they were planning something. Then he told me why: "Last June, just before school let out, I saw Gruder teasing a cat. He had it trapped in a wire mesh trash basket and was poking at it with a stick. I said my ESP told me he was going to get scratched. He looked around to answer back, and at that moment the cat scratched his arm—really drew blood—and then ran off. I just kept walking, and Gruder yelled after me, 'I'll get you for this.' But he doesn't really bother me. He just has a few more problems than most people."

Then McGee asked me if I wanted to come over Saturday morning and meet his father—in person! Naturally I said yes. For one thing it would give me a chance to learn something about computers.

I couldn't help but admire McGee's lack of anxiety about what Gruder and his friends might do. Was McGee a totally fearless person, I wondered, or did his ESP tell him that there was nothing to worry about? And what could I do to help if he needed protection? The two of us together would be no match for those guys. Maybe I could shadow them and then scream for help if they started to beat up McGee. If only I could bring Loser to school. Loser is basically as gentle as a lamb, but he's very big, and if I needed protection I knew Loser could scare the pants off of Hank Gruder with one long, low growl.

By the time Friday came, I could hardly concentrate on anything at school. To make things worse, Hank Gruder kept grinning at me as if we shared some special secret.

I had decided that, since I couldn't bring Loser to school, I would try to avoid Gruder and his buddies and shadow McGee home. Then, if there was any way I could help, I would. Finally the bell sounded—the last class of the day was over, and I was the first kid out of the school building. As I walked down the steps I was surprised to see a police car waiting. One of the two officers got out and came toward me.

"Glad to see you again, son," he said.

"Who *me?*" I said, confused.

"No, me," said a familiar voice. It was McGee, coming down the steps behind me.

"I thought you might be here in case there was any action," he said, "and I appreciate that. But we have more important things to do. These officers are picking me up be-

47

cause I've agreed to help the police with a serious problem. Angela Kimmel has been kidnapped!"

Angela Kimmel was in my science class. I'd heard her family was very rich, but she seemed just like any other kid—not one bit uppity or snobby. It was quite a shock to hear she'd been kidnapped, but I had to get over it fast. McGee wanted me to come with him. We'd brought our bikes to school, so we loaded them in the trunk of the squad car. A few moments later we were headed for police headquarters, or so I thought.

But the car turned the other way, toward Greenport Heights. "We're going to Roy Kimmel's house," said McGee. Then he proceeded to fill me in on the facts: Angela's parents were killed in an auto accident when she was only three years old, and she was brought up by her uncle, Roy Kimmel. He was the richest man in Greenport, but that never did Angela much good. He traveled a lot and was so busy making money that Angela pretty much had only maids and butlers for a family.

When I'd met her, Angela had seemed kind of unhappy; after what McGee told me, I could see why.

"Old man Kimmel doesn't let anyone get in his way, including his own family," McGee said. "I never thought I'd want to help that man, but with Angela missing, I'm hoping to do just that. She disappeared on her way to school this morning—someplace between her house and the bus stop, which is about a ten-minute walk away. I helped the police find a 'kidnapped' child once before—Jim Brewer's little sister. It turned out she hadn't been kidnapped at all. She'd fallen into a storm sewer."

McGee stopped talking as the police car started up a long winding driveway leading to a huge brick house with about eight chimneys. The grounds were neatly trimmed and landscaped with stately trees. We passed what I'd guess you'd call a caretaker's cottage, then a guest house set by a brook that tumbled over a rock ledge like a miniature Niagara Falls. Beyond the main house I could see a horse barn and tennis courts.

Our car pulled up near the front door, and we followed the officers inside. A butler showed us into an oak-paneled library.

Mr. Kimmel, a bald man with steel-rimmed spectacles and a dark three-piece suit, was waiting for us, along with a man I later learned was his chauffeur, Benny. Also present was a tall white-haired man, Inspector Chadsy of the Police Department. Chadsy introduced McGee to Mr. Kimmel, and McGee introduced me as his "associate." Kimmel shook my hand with a grip that reminded me of Hank Gruder, then told us all to sit down and make ourselves comfortable.

"Well," said Chadsy, "this is it." He handed McGee a sheet of paper with cut-out magazine letters pasted on it. I read over McGee's shoulder.

LEAVE $50,000 AT 5:00 P.M. BY THE FENCE AT INVERNESS ROAD. IF THE POLICE INTERFERE, YOU WILL NEVER SEE ANGELA AGAIN.

"I intend to pay it, of course," Kimmel said. "Then I want you to arrest Avery before he tries anything else."

Chadsy flushed and asked one of his men if he had anything on Avery yet. I guessed he meant the Mr. Avery who owned the boatyard at the head of the harbor. Just a week before he'd caught me fishing off his dock, and instead of getting mad, he'd just said "Good luck."

"What's Avery got to do with it?" McGee asked.

Kimmel looked him in the eye and said, "The ransom is

49

the amount that Avery owes my bank on a loan that's due a few days from now. I'm sure he can't pay it off, and that means we'll have to foreclose on his boatyard and put it up for sale. It's obvious that Avery kidnapped Angela in a desperate attempt to get the fifty thousand dollars."

Kimmel walked across the room, opened a wall safe, and pulled out more stacks of money than I'd ever seen in my life. While we all watched, he briskly counted it, stuffed it in a brown paper bag, and stapled the bag shut. Then he turned to his chauffeur and said, "Benny, deliver this as instructed." As Benny left, he continued. "From what I know of Avery, he won't harm Angela as long as he can get the money to save his boatyard. But, if he's cornered . . ." Kimmel paced up and down, wringing his hands. Then he stopped abruptly in front of the inspector. "Remember, until Angela is safely back, no police interference."

Chadsy replied in an even tone of voice, "We have no intention of jeopardizing the child, Mr. Kimmel, but keep in mind we don't take orders from you."

McGee seemed to take no notice of this. He was staring out the window at the harbor. "It's getting near the end of the season," he said quietly. "I guess you'll be hauling up your boat soon, Mr. Kimmel."

"I haven't sailed since I was your age. I used to race, but . . . look, you're here because you're supposed to be some sort of psychic. Do you know where Angela is?"

"Not exactly, sir. But I have some ideas I'd like to check out. I'll let you know when I have something more concrete. Come on, Matt."

Kimmel scowled and we made a quick exit. As we got our bicycles from the trunk of the squad car, I asked McGee which part of town he thought we should check first.

"This one," he said. "Let's have a look around the grounds. You take the stables and the tennis courts. I'll check the cottage and the guest house. Meet me down at the end of the drive when you're done."

The stables were behind the main house and the tennis courts off to the side. I found a couple of old tennis balls in the tall grass, but didn't see anything that seemed related to Angela's disappearance, so I pedaled back down to the end of the drive. McGee was already there, and I remember thinking he looked rather pleased with himself.

"Didn't find a thing, except these." I tossed the tennis balls at him.

"I didn't find much more."

"What did you mean when you told Kimmel you had a few ideas?"

He answered slowly. "I'm not sure there's been a kidnap-

51

ping. I don't think we have to worry about Angela, and I think we should wait right here. I have a feeling she's going to be returned very soon. Let's hide behind these bushes and lay low for a while." There was something about his tone that made me hold my questions.

So we waited. About an hour later, we heard a car climbing the hill at full speed. It skidded to a stop at the end of the driveway. As we clambered from the bushes and ran toward the sound, we heard the car accelerating down the road.

McGee yelled, "There she is!"

Angela Kimmel was blindfolded and bound hand and foot and yet she struggled toward us, hopping like someone in a sack race. We untied her and held her up while she rubbed her ankles where they'd been chafed by the ropes. Her hair was a mess, and I could see she'd been crying.

"Matt? McGee?" Her voice was shaky.

"Are you all right?" I asked.

"I guess so. No one hurt me. But it was horrible. They gagged and bound me and blindfolded me—I never knew what they were going to do. They wouldn't even talk to me." She started crying.

"It's okay. You're safe now," McGee said.

Angela brushed her hair back from her face and smiled a little.

"You never saw who did it?" McGee asked.

Angela shook her head. Then she seemed to notice where she was for the first time. "Why did this happen? Why did they bring me back?"

"I guess because your uncle paid the ransom," I told her.

"He paid a ransom for me? He's never done anything for me. He's always been too busy making money to care about me—or anyone else."

After Angela calmed down a little she told us how she'd been seized from behind while walking to the bus stop, and how she had been blindfolded so fast she didn't even get a glimpse of the kidnappers.

"Were they rough with you?" I asked.

"As soon as they saw I couldn't escape, they treated me okay," she said. "They even gave me soft pillows to lie against. But the terrible thing was, I never knew what they'd do next."

"Do you have any idea who kidnapped you?" McGee said.

Angela smiled weakly and shook her head. She looked kind of pale, and I could tell it would take a long time for her to recover from her ordeal.

"Did you see anything at all the whole time?" McGee asked.

Again she shook her head.

"Do you have any idea where they took you?"

"Not really."

"Hear any unusual sounds?"

"No."

"Any *usual* sounds?"

Angela laughed. "Well, the car traffic." Then her eyes brightened. "I heard running water, like a little waterfall."

McGee thought for a few seconds, then he said, "Tell me, does your Uncle Roy have anyone working for him that you might suspect?"

"Uncle Roy's chauffeur—Benny. He's shifty-eyed and I've never liked him. He lives in the caretaker's cottage and has worked for Uncle Roy for years."

"You said your kidnappers never spoke. Was there any other way you could tell if one of them was Benny?"

Angela stared into space, then shook her head.

54

McGee looked at me, but I didn't know what to say. I was just trying to follow the conversation.

"Matt, would you walk Angela home? I have an errand to do. Angela, may I borrow your bracelet for a short while? I can't explain now, but I think it might help me find out who kidnapped you."

Angela looked dazed, but she slipped off her bracelet and handed it to McGee. We got our bikes; then I steered Angela back to the house while McGee pedaled down the drive.

Of course everyone was overjoyed to see Angela. Inspector Chadsy started in right away asking her questions. The butler telephoned the doctor to come over and take a look at her. (I guess when you're that rich they still make house calls.) A maid brought in ice cream, cookies, and ginger ale—enough for me, too. Then a call came through from McGee. He had returned home and asked me to meet him there.

I said good-bye to Angela and the others. As I left, Chadsy put a hand on my shoulder and said, "Thanks, son. Tell ESP McGee we're grateful to have Angela back, but we still don't have the case solved. Do you think McGee is still interested in helping us?"

"I believe so, sir," I replied. "I'll certainly give him your message." After another painful handshake and brief good-bye from Kimmel, I was on my way.

Chapter
Seven

WHEN I reached McGee's house, he had a couple of huge sandwiches ready for us: leftover roast beef, avocado, ham, cheese, sprouts, mushrooms, tomatoes, and just about everything else in the fridge. "I called your folks, and they said it's okay for you to stay for dinner and overnight," he told me. We polished off the sandwiches and were just starting in on some strawberry ice cream when McGee's parents walked in.

"You must be Matt," said his mother. "We've been looking forward to meeting you."

I gulped down my spoonful of ice cream and started to get up, while McGee's father leaned over and shook hands. Then Mrs. McGee sat down at the table, and Mr. McGee went to the fridge and began making a sandwich identical to the ones McGee had made.

"I'm amazed—there's still a little ice cream left in the freezer," Mr. McGee said. His voice sounded exactly like it had on the computer.

McGee told his parents about the kidnapping, but once they learned that Angela was okay, they didn't seem all that interested. His mother started talking about the intelligence experiments she was doing with a giant octopus she had on loan from Washington, and his father wanted to know what I knew about computers.

Not much, I had to admit.

"Well," he said cheerfully, "spend some time with us, and you'll learn all you need to know."

"I'll take you up on that," I said.

"Only we can't start now," put in McGee, "because we have some work to do."

We excused ourselves and went to the computer room where McGee started punching away at a terminal. "Dad recently helped the town computerize all public records of landholdings, taxes, zoning, building codes and practically everything else that's a matter of public record. I have the access code, so instead of poring through a lot of dusty books in the Town Hall we can do our detective work right here."

I watched while McGee called up information on local property: tax assessments, records of who held the deeds to which pieces of land, a map of waterfront property lines, and, finally, a chart of the harbor that gave channel locations and depths up to a mile beyond shore.

"McGee, what's all this for?"

"One of those papers on Kimmel's desk was a coastal chart—an odd thing to have if you don't sail, don't you agree?"

57

Before I had a chance to answer, he was calling up more information. Finally, he was finished and we went up to bed.

The next morning he got me up early. "We've got to get to Avery's boatyard. We can grab something for breakfast and eat it on the way."

"Why so early?" I was barely awake enough to talk.

"It's almost certain the police will have a search warrant by this morning, and we have to get there before they get inside the office."

We biked at top speed down to the waterfront. Even though it was mostly downhill, I was out of breath when we reached the boatyard. We approached on foot from the side, keeping hidden. The yard wasn't open for business yet, but a police car was parked out front. "They're waiting for Avery to show up," McGee said. "Do you think you could be a distraction?"

"A what?"

"I want to check out the office. There's a small window in back, facing the boat shed. I'm pretty sure I can jimmy it open and crawl through. If you'll just happen to fall off the end of the dock, that will buy me some time while they rescue you. If they don't, you can always swim to shore."

The morning air was still cool. I looked at the water and shivered. I'm a pretty good swimmer, but it wasn't going to be warm.

"Then what?"

"They'll probably bawl you out and give you a warning. Keep them busy as long as you can. Then meet me back at my house."

Falling off the dock was the last thing I wanted to do, but I knew that McGee was counting on me. I walked calmly past

58

the policemen and then along the edge of the dock, pretending to be fascinated by something in the water.

"Hey, come off of there," one of the cops yelled. But it was too late. I'd already "slipped." *Splash.* I could hear the cops running along the dock, and I held onto a piling as if I couldn't make it to shore. It must have been ten minutes before they'd fished me out and given me the predictable lecture. I stole a glance toward the office. There was no sign of McGee. Wet clothes and all, I pedaled to his house. He was waiting for me at the door with a big grin on his face and a bathrobe for me to wear while my clothes were in the dryer.

"Take a look at this, Matt." He pointed to a familiar-looking paper bag on the hall table.

"The ransom money?"

"Right. We're about to deliver it back to Mr. Kimmel."

"You found it in the boatyard?"

"Right again—in Avery's desk."

"Then Avery's guilty?"

"The police would probably think so, which is why—if anyone asks—we have to say that we found it on East Meadow Road, near the golf course."

"We do?" I asked.

"Yes, I think so," said McGee, "although it may not come to that. I hope I can hold off on returning the bag till the case is solved, but I don't like being responsible for so much money. By the way, that was a first-class distraction, Terrell."

I liked hearing that. "What now?" I asked.

"I've arranged for everyone to meet at Kimmel's house in half an hour. With a little luck we'll have this case wrapped up by sunset in Bermuda."

I didn't know when sunset in Bermuda would be, but there isn't time to question McGee on everything.

As soon as my clothes were dry, we were on our way, pedaling to Greenport Heights and then up the long winding drive to Kimmel's house. When we arrived, McGee asked me to wait five minutes—he had a quick errand to perform. I watched him bike toward the caretaker's cottage. Another mysterious McGee maneuver. He was back in five minutes on the nose, and soon we were all assembled in the library—Kimmel, Inspector Chadsy and two assistant detectives, Angela, and Hargraves the butler.

"All right, young fellow," Kimmel barked, "I'm putting up with a lot of nuisance because of your astounding reputation. I don't intend to be at your beck and call, so tell us what you have been up to and what you have learned, *if anything.*"

"I've been solving the case," McGee said, holding up Angela's silver and enamel bracelet. "Do you recognize this, Mr. Kimmel?"

"It looks like the bracelet Angela always wears," said Mr. Kimmel, "but I fail to see its importance."

"Where did you find it, McGee?" Chadsy asked sharply. "Do you know where Angela was held?"

"I do," McGee replied, "and I know who kidnapped her."

"Who?" Kimmel's voice was filled with scorn.

"Your chauffeur, Benny," McGee said.

"That's absurd. He's been a trusted servant of mine for years." Kimmel laughed—but it was a nervous laugh.

"How do you know it was Benny?" Inspector Chadsy said, glaring at McGee in frustration.

"He told me," McGee said simply.

Everyone gasped. At that moment the door banged open and Benny himself strode in. His face was red with anger.

"So you tried to have me take the rap," he said, his eyes burning with rage. "If I'm going to suffer for this, you're going to suffer with me!"

"Shut up, Benny!" Kimmel barked.

"So you did do it?" Chadsy demanded.

"He did it!" Benny screamed, shaking his fist at Kimmel. "And he *made* me help him. He was blackmailing me because he knew I was wanted on a gambling rap."

"You fool!" Kimmel was on his feet screaming back at Benny. "You could have gone a long way with me."

"You'll still be going a long way together," Chadsy said dryly, "—all the way to prison."

It took about two seconds for the detectives to hustle Kimmel and Benny into a squad car, leaving McGee and me alone with Inspector Chadsy and Angela.

"I'm amazed that Kimmel would kidnap his own niece," Chadsy said to McGee, "but I'm even more amazed that you got Benny to confess and Kimmel to panic. Where *did* you find Angela's bracelet?"

"She loaned it to me after she was let loose," McGee answered matter-of-factly. "They kept you prisoner in the guest cottage," he said to Angela. "I was sure of it when you mentioned hearing the waterfall. Benny and your uncle were terribly afraid they'd left some clue there. They'd been very careful, but they couldn't be *sure* they had been careful enough. They were already suspicious of each other when the police didn't find the ransom money in Avery's office. And when I told Benny that Matt and I had found your bracelet in the guest cottage and that Kimmel had accused him of the crime, it was enough to throw him into a panic."

"Well, I'll be . . ." said Chadsy. "Maybe you don't have ESP. Maybe you're just a great actor."

"Or maybe the secret to being a great actor is having ESP," McGee replied. "If you want to convince someone he's seeing the real thing—not just an act—you have to know exactly what tone of voice and which gestures to use. Apparently, I convinced Benny."

"That's certain, at least," said Chadsy. "Now how did you know Kimmel was involved?"

McGee explained how the data from the computer showed that Kimmel had been acquiring waterfront property to build a huge condominium and marina. He had already bought the land around the boatyard, but Avery refused to sell his piece.

"I figured that Kimmel lied when he said Avery couldn't pay off the loan. And when he couldn't buy the property *or* foreclose on it, he hatched the kidnapping plan. It was a desperate move, but he was determined to get the boatyard—even if he had to use his niece and ruin Avery to do it."

The next ten minutes were a mixture of confusion, celebration, tears, and telephone calls. McGee turned over the money to Chadsy; then he spent quite a while talking to Angela. He must have said the right things, because by the time we left she seemed pretty calm—even happy.

"One thing I don't get," I said as we biked toward home. "How did you know Angela would be set free so soon?"

"I figured that Kimmel didn't really want to harm her," McGee replied. "He only wanted to hold her long enough to create the crime he intended to pin on Avery."

That satisfied me until I realized he hadn't explained how he knew exactly where and when Angela would be released. I didn't want to push him on the subject of his ESP, so instead I asked, "What will happen to Angela now that her uncle's going to be behind bars for a while?"

"She's going to live with her Aunt Sara in California, and she's really happy about it. She's always wanted to live with her, but her uncle had legal custody."

I was glad to hear that but sorry Angela would be moving away. I liked her.

Chapter
Eight

MONDAY I waited awhile after school and watched McGee head home, untroubled as usual. Later I saw Gruder and some other guys playing Frisbee. I guessed that maybe they'd heard about McGee helping the police solve the Angela Kimmel case and had decided they could only get in trouble by harassing him.

I walked home with Nick Cracus, a kid I'd become friendly with in history class, and told him about Gruder and his goons.

"I wouldn't feel too secure, if I were McGee," Nick said. "Gruder and those other guys may lay low for a while, but they're mean and I've heard them talking. Sooner or later they're going to get McGee."

Nick sounded very convincing, though in the little while

I'd known him I'd noticed that he tended to exaggerate a lot in order to sound more interesting. Maybe he knew what he was talking about; maybe not.

Of course, I made sure I attended the ESP Club meeting after school that Friday. About ten or fifteen kids were there, including Nick Cracus, Doug Viladis, and Jack Hopper. To my relief, Hank Gruder and his friends didn't show up. But Nina Ravinsky was there with her friend Luanna-Lee Leonni. (That's her name, no kidding.) I knew it was going to be a lively meeting. I had no idea what Nina would say but I knew she'd say something.

Mr. Maynard cleared his throat and began the meeting. "I started this club because the possibilities of ESP are very exciting. Together, I hope we can explore the various forms of psychic abilities and learn to recognize our own powers."

Nina didn't waste any time. "I think it's all silly," she said. "There's no hard proof that ESP exists."

"Do you have proof that it doesn't?" Mr. Maynard returned.

Terrific, I thought, this club is going to be one long debate with Nina Ravinsky.

But Mr. Maynard went on before Nina had a chance to reply. "Actually, ESP *is* a difficult phenomenon to prove, especially under laboratory conditions. The term ESP has become a catchall for several different types of psychic ability. It might refer to the ability to send and receive thoughts, or to feel something undetectable to the five senses, or to move an object without touching it. Some scientists believe that we all have psychic powers to a degree. Certain people are simply more aware of these powers or have developed them to a greater extent. One purpose of this club is to see if any of us

65

has ESP. Have any of you ever had what you'd call a psychic experience?"

We looked around the room at each other, but no one said anything. Finally, Nick Cracus cautiously raised his hand.

"Come on, Cracus," said Jack Hopper. "We won't laugh."

Nick hesitated. He looked a little spooked. Then, in a voice not much louder than a whisper, he began:

"Nothing like this ever happened to me before. Two years ago, I had a dream that I was in New York City. I'd never been there, but somehow I knew it was New York. I was on a narrow street filled with shops. I saw this little lane that curved off the street, and I followed it till I came to a real dusty storefront window. The sign above the door said, 'P. McFarland, Stamps.' Well, you know me and my stamp collection. In the dream I owned a c18 Graf Zeppelin. I rang the bell and an old guy wearing striped suspenders let me in. He showed me an album he was working on, and I showed him my stamp. We looked at his stamps for a while and then I left."

"What's a c18 Graf Zeppelin?" asked Jack.

"It's a 1933 fifty-cent stamp that's worth almost two hundred dollars! Anyway, right after that dream I woke up—feeling lousy because I didn't really own that stamp."

"So?" demanded Nina.

"So," Nick continued, "the next year my sister went to college in New York. When I visited her, we took a walk through Greenwich Village. And I swear, we wound up on the exact same street that was in my dream. I headed straight for P. McFarland's stamp shop and rang the bell. He opened the door; he was wearing those same striped suspenders and that same album was open on his desk. But this time when he saw me, he turned a little pale and said, 'I've wondered if you'd come back for it. You brought it here to show me almost a year ago and forgot to take it with you.' Then he picked up the c18 and gave it to me."

"Are you sure you didn't leave it there, just as he said?" Luanna-Lee wanted to know.

Nick just shrugged. "Do you think I wouldn't remember visiting New York City for the first time in my life?"

"You're just making this up!" Doug almost shouted.

"What Nick just described," Mr. Maynard broke in, "is an example of precognition, the ability to sense what's going to occur in the future."

"It seems like a lot more than that," said Jack. "It seems weird."

"It seems *unbelievable*," Nina added.

Everyone laughed, and Mr. Maynard had to rap on the table to get us to quiet down. "Well, there is something here that goes even beyond ESP: the fact that Mr. McFarland *saw* Nick and saved the stamp for him long before Nick actually visited the shop. That might come under the heading of 'out-of-body experiences.' But it's so deep into the realm of the unknown that I don't think we can even begin to discuss it yet."

"Don't they believe that happens in India—with gurus?" I asked, remembering something Dad had told me.

But Mr. Maynard held up his hands. "Let's just try to understand regular ESP first, shall we?" Then he talked on quite a bit about precognition and how it often occurs during dreams. He said that if any of us thought we were precognitive, we should start keeping a record of our dreams.

"Do you think McGee's precognitive?" Jack asked. "And where is he, anyway?"

"Well, I'm sorry he didn't choose to come to our first meeting," said Mr. Maynard, "but I'm hopeful he'll join us at

67

some point. Obviously it would be very interesting to hear about some of his experiences. But whether or not he shows up, we'll be discussing some of his achievements and trying to decide if he used ESP and how it might have worked."

"May I make an observation, Mr. Maynard?"

Oh, oh, I thought, here we go. Though she'd been fairly quiet so far, Nina Ravinsky was now on her feet, holding a bunch of papers and notes.

"Why certainly, Nina," Mr. Maynard said.

"First of all," she began, "there's another way to look at this ESP. No offense, Nick, but I think you must have had amnesia after your first trip to New York. And as for McGee—his detective work is based on logic, ingenuity, and a lot of luck."

"What about that earthquake he predicted?" asked Nick, sounding a little hurt.

Nina had an answer for everything. "That sounds impressive until you realize that earthquakes can often be predicted by observing animal behavior. Some scientists say that animals may be sensitive to electrical charges in the atmosphere. We know they hear vibrations beyond the range normally audible to humans. Maybe McGee saw animals behaving strangely before the quake. Or maybe his hearing is more sensitive than normal. He might have unusual talents, but that's not the same as ESP."

"Thank you, Nina," Mr. Maynard said. "Both you and Nick have given us plenty to think about for our next meeting."

"Do you personally believe in ESP, Mr. Maynard?" Sue Tuttle asked.

"I won't answer your question now," he answered, smiling, "but those who stay in the club all year will find out."

"Will we find out by ESP or because you tell us?" Jack Hopper asked.

Everyone laughed, but Mr. Maynard kept a straight face and replied, "That's a good question, Jack."

"I think he *does* believe in ESP," Nick whispered to me, "otherwise he wouldn't have said it was a good question."

"Maybe," I said.

The meeting was over. Nina walked out, looking smug as ever. "Mr. Maynard didn't prove a thing," she told me, "and neither did Nick."

I was completely confused. Nina's theory about McGee made sense. Of course he used logic, he was too smart not to. But I thought about the way he'd been with the animals on the farm and the way he'd handled the Angela Kimmel case—the way he just seemed to *know* things. And I thought about Nick's dream. Now I know Nick can tell a pretty good story, but somehow that one sounded real to me.

Chapter
Nine

I DON'T know if it had anything to do with Nina's performance, but that night McGee phoned to say he was going up to Boston with his parents for the weekend—something about an important meeting at M.I.T. I didn't see him much the following week, and everyone was involved with other things—sports and homework mostly. Even Nina seemed subdued, and Hank Gruder got caught smoking on school grounds so he had something else to think about for a while.

Things settled down to normal until one day about a week or so later. I'd spent the afternoon playing touch football and didn't get home until almost six, but Mom said "no problem" because Dad was delayed getting home from the office. She was fixing dinner and Emily was sitting on a stool in the corner, very sulky and quiet. I could tell she was in trouble with Mom over something.

They were having what Mom called a "discussion." We have discussions whenever one of us does something wrong. Whoever's in trouble sits down—usually in the kitchen—and Mom talks. There are long periods of silence while Mom goes about her work, but if you try to leave early, she'll say, "Just a minute, we're not through with our discussion yet." So it's pretty much as if she said, "Sit in the corner for an hour and think about what you've done."

I tended to get into trouble a good deal more than Emily, so naturally I was curious to know what was going on. Usually I'd wait till I could talk to Mom or Emily alone, but for some reason I was feeling bold that day. So I just asked right out, "What did Emily do wrong?"

Emily just kept looking out the window and Mom glared at me ferociously, so I knew it must be pretty bad. Then she stood there a minute as if trying to decide whether or not what Emily had done was too awful to mention. Finally she said, "Emily spent half the afternoon at the Video Arcade, even though we have a strict rule she's not to set foot in there."

"Oh, is that all?" I said.

"All!" Now Mom was mad at me.

"It wasn't *half the afternoon*," Emily blurted out. "It was about *twenty* minutes. Besides I had Loser with me."

"Loser!" Mom was really getting warmed up. "What good does that do? That makes it all the worse because you were supposed to be taking Loser on a run through the park. A big dog like that needs exercise! Instead you shut him up in a dark, noisy, unhealthy, unsavory dump like the Video Arcade!"

"I didn't shut him up!" Emily said with real conviction.

71

"Loser has a *penchant* for the Video Arcade. He's fascinated by all the moving lights and sounds. I couldn't get him to leave!"

Mom stood with her hands on her hips, shaking her head.

But Emily was so wound up, she just kept talking. "You should see him. When there's really good action on a machine, Loser goes over and gets up on his hind legs and sort of growls in a real strange way. He sounds as if he's electronic or something . . ."

I could see Mom's lips twitching, and I knew she was trying to keep from laughing. Emily knew it, too; she looked up with pleading eyes. "Besides, Mom, ESP McGee was there. He was analyzing the programming of the video games. It was very educational."

"Those games are about as educational as playing a slot machine or shooting craps. And the money kids pour into those machines. Personally, if I wanted to throw away quarters, I'd rather go to the beach and skip them into Long Island Sound."

"But it *would* be educational seeing what McGee was doing," I put in. "Mr. McGee has been designing a three-dimensional space game simulation using holography, and McGee is helping him."

"Maybe so," Mom said, "but I don't think for a minute that you're getting educated at the Video Arcade. Emily, you're not to go there again, do you understand?"

"Even if Loser *drags* me there?" Emily persisted.

"NO!"

"But Matt goes."

"Matt's older." Mom had used that argument before, and I really wish she wouldn't. It makes Emily hate me. Well, not *really* hate me, because we get along pretty well most of the time. But it does make her mad.

Dad pulled into the drive, and Emily was up from her stool in a flash. "Here's Dad," she called, opening the back door to meet him.

"You really shouldn't waste your time and money in that arcade either," Mom said to me. Then she turned and followed Emily. The fight was over and I was relieved that Dad hadn't arrived any earlier. Sometimes he'd make things worse by trying to turn a fight into a debate and judge who had the best argument. For some reason that didn't work too well with the kinds of fights Emily and Mom and I had.

The next afternoon it was my turn to take Loser on a walk. When we got to the park, I let the big dummy off his leash. I'd brought along an old tennis ball and threw it as far as I could. Loser took off after the ball, then changed direction and grabbed a dirty crumpled milk shake container and dashed back to me.

"What about the ball, Loser?"

Loser wagged his tail. One thing about this dog—he's too dumb to know how dumb he is, so he stays as happy as a dog can be.

"Well, at least you're helping fight the litter problem," I said, dropping the container in a trash can. Loser rubbed up against me, pleased, then started trotting off toward Front Street.

"Loser, come back here!" I wished I'd gotten his leash back on, but I hadn't, and when Loser decides not to come when you call, there's nothing to do but go after him. So I trotted along, too. Thank goodness he got across the road safely, but I didn't catch up to him till he was halfway down

73

Front Street, standing with his tail wagging a mile a minute in front of the Video Arcade.

I couldn't help but laugh. I snapped on his leash and reached in my pocket; just one quarter there. Well, why not, I thought, and we went inside. I wanted to play Strike Force but Loser wanted to check out something called Armageddon, which had about a million lights that blinked every time a player blew up a planet. It took me almost ten minutes to get Loser over to Strike Force. Then he sat quietly while I played.

Only 2,300 points. I've done a lot better.

It wasn't till I'd finished the game that I looked around and noticed Hank Gruder and one of his goon friends, Phil Paxton, lurking in the back of the room. Have you ever seen those signs that say "No Loitering"? Well, if anyone was ever loitering, it was Hank and Phil.

Hank glared and then started toward me. I was glad I had Loser along. But Hank didn't come on in his usual style.

"Hey, how're you doing?" he said, sounding almost sincere.

"Okay. How about you?"

"Your friend McGee around?"

"Haven't seen him lately."

Phil had stayed back, giving me the feeling that Hank wanted to talk to me alone. I figured something was on Hank's mind, but he didn't seem to know what to say next.

"You know whether McGee is going to be here today?" he finally asked.

"No, I really don't."

Hank fidgeted, then he said, "You know, there's something funny going on. I don't know whether I ought to tell you but maybe I ought to."

"Yeah, what is it?"

75

"There's a man who's been hanging around school—about thirty years old. He got talking to me one day and asked me whether I knew ESP McGee and what I thought of him. I told him I didn't think much of him and we talked some more and then he asked me where McGee hangs out and I told him sometimes he hangs out here. Then the guy gives me twenty bucks and tells me to hang out here and all I have to do is phone him when McGee comes in and I'll get twenty more. So I said that sounds good to me, but now I get the feeling there's something weird about all this and I don't want to be involved anymore, but if I don't wait around here and do what I said I was going to do—and just keep the twenty bucks—this guy will catch up with me . . ."

Hank had run out of breath. He probably had never talked so much in his life. He looked at me with pleading eyes. All I could think of was how weird it was that this tough guy, this big scary bully, was scared to death himself. And not only that—he was appealing to a skinny kid like me for help. I was beginning to enjoy seeing Gruder in a fix, but then it hit me: this was a serious problem. It looked as if someone was out to get ESP McGee, and not just an eighth-grade bully.

"I think you should tell the police," I said.

Gruder shook his head. "No way. I don't want to get mixed up with those turkeys."

"That's the only way you might *avoid* getting mixed up," I said. "Come on, Loser, it's time for your supper."

I pulled my good-for-nothing dog away from Attack Command and dragged him outside. "Let's jog," I said and broke into a trot with Loser reined in beside me. I'd decided to stop by McGee's house on the way home and tell him about my conversation with Hank Gruder.

But first I ran—literally—into Nina Ravinsky. The three

of us wound up on the sidewalk all tangled together in Loser's leash. Nina looked like she wanted to scream but didn't say anything.

"Look, I'm sorry," I said, and wondered why I always wind up apologizing for my dog. "Let me help you up."

"I'm fine," she said, getting up on her own.

Only Loser looked a bit shaky.

"Going to see the great McGee?" she asked.

"As a matter of fact I am. Must be your ESP that told you that."

"Deductive reasoning," she said but she was smiling. "Tell McGee I've also deduced that he'd better stay away from Hank Gruder. I've heard Hank ask a couple of kids if they've seen McGee, and I think he's up to no good." Then she actually patted Loser's head before she walked off.

Ten minutes later I was ringing McGee's doorbell. No one answered, but I waited awhile, thinking that he might be in the computer room or that the McGees might be having an early dinner. It was already starting to get dark out. I was about to give up when McGee opened the door.

"Hi," he said. "My parents are out for dinner and I didn't want to open the door until I saw who it was from the upstairs porch. I have a feeling someone is after me."

"I'm afraid you may be right," I said. "That's why I'm here."

Right then a stocky man leaped out of the shrubbery. He had a baseball cap pulled over his forehead and the high collar of his trench coat turned up, so all I could see of his face was a crooked nose and bushy beard. In one hand he held a long barreled revolver.

"Hold it right there, you two. Don't move."

McGee and I froze. Loser started wagging his tail. "Why

77

didn't you bark?" I snarled at him. I was almost madder at Loser than I was at the gunman.

"Keep that dog away from me. I'd just as soon shoot him as look at him—and that goes for you, too." He waved his gun in front of my face. "Now get him in the house. Then both of you get in that car." He motioned toward a maroon Toyota that had pulled up the drive.

By now Loser's tail had stopped wagging. He stood with his head cocked to one side looking curiously at the gunman. I could tell he was slowly beginning to realize that something was wrong. I was glad of that but fearful the gunman might start shooting.

"Didn't you hear me? Get that dog inside the house!"

"But it's not his house," I said.

"Get him in there!" The gunman sounded almost panicky.

I shoved Loser inside and closed the door behind him. At the same time I felt a sharp rap as the gunman slapped the pistol across my back. *"In the car—fast,"* he said.

I wished McGee were already a T'ai-chi master who could get us out of this. But it didn't work that way. Reluctantly, he and I walked to the car. The gunman shoved us into the back seat and climbed in between us. The car backed out of the drive, took off around the corner, and turned onto Haven Avenue.

"Where are you taking us?" McGee asked in a firm voice.

The driver looked back at him over his shoulder. "You ought to know—you're the one with ESP." They both laughed.

"I don't have ESP," I blurted out, "and *I'd* like to know where you're taking us!"

The answer came back fast. "The Prout's Neck Nuclear Power Plant."

"Who are you and what do you want?" I could hear my voice shaking.

The gunman turned on me, sneering. "You talk nice to us, sonny," he said, flickering his gun in my face. "Don't ask questions, and you won't get hurt—understand?"

Suddenly he jabbed the gun barrel into my shoulder. I let out a yelp as a sharp pain radiated down my arm.

"You don't need to do that," McGee said evenly.

"Not anymore, do I, sonny?" The gunman laughed uncontrollably until his partner stopped him short.

"Cut it, Willie. Get down to business."

The driver wheeled around another corner at high speed and turned onto Shore Road. We were no longer headed toward the nuclear plant, but I didn't say anything. No need to give them directions!

"Obviously you don't expect a warm welcome at the front gate," said McGee.

"Obviously," said the driver. "You see, Willie, if you had half the brains this kid has, you might amount to something!"

Willie looked sullen but remained silent while the driver turned down a dirt driveway leading to a small cluttered boatyard. Across the narrow opening to Greenport Harbor loomed the large spindle-shaped concrete structure of the power plant. I didn't need ESP to know that we were going there by boat. I wondered what McGee was thinking— whether he had any plans for our escape and whether his powers could help us. Then I wondered what my parents would do when I didn't show up for dinner. They'd probably ground me. I almost laughed. Here I was, kidnapped by lunatics and worrying about being grounded.

The Toyota stopped abruptly behind a sagging tin boat shed. The driver turned off the ignition and headlights and wheeled around to face us. "You've already met Willie," he said. "My name is Z."

I was waiting for McGee to say "You'll never get away with this" or something like that, but he remained silent, and so did I.

"We are ordinary American citizens, working for a living to make ends meet," said Z. "Only thing is—our boss has expensive tastes. He sometimes needs a little extra cash, and right now he needs ten million dollars—tonight."

"I only have a buck fifty on me," McGee said.

"Very funny," Z replied.

If McGee could talk back to these guys, so could I. "Can't you just rob a bank or something?" I said.

Willie pressed the muzzle of his gun up against my forehead. "Banks don't have that kind of money lying around," he said.

"What Willie is trying to tell you," Z said, "is that to get that kind of money you have to be willing to blow up a nuclear plant."

McGee looked at me and softly uttered a single word: "Terrorists."

Chapter
Ten

THE next half hour was like a nightmare in which strange things happen to you and you can't control what's taking place so you don't feel human, you feel like an object—like a crinkled up hunk of paper thrown into a roaring river. The terrorists yanked us out of the car and shoved us into a rowboat. McGee and I squeezed together in the bowseat, Willie rowed, and Z sat in the stern holding a small silver gun that glittered when the light hit it. Every once in a while he told Willie to pull more on one oar or the other as we rowed toward the huge concrete structure on the opposite shore.

Silently, in the darkness, we glided up to a stone jetty at the end of Prout's Neck. For a moment we were lighted up by the floodlights around the plant, and I wondered if a guard would spot us. Then we were in the dark again as Willie beached the boat in the shadow of some trees growing near the shore.

"Everyone out," said Z.

"Any noise and you're dead," Willie added, his voice shaking. I took some hope from his being nervous. We stepped ankle deep in the cold water and then plodded up the beach. The only sound McGee and I made was from the water sloshing out of our sneakers.

Z marched us silently and swiftly across an open area toward the containment building. For a few minutes we were right under the floodlights, but if there were any guards, they must have been patrolling another area. The plant was protected by a high fence and heavy security at the front gate, but it seemed that anyone coming in late at night by sea had a good chance of reaching the building itself undetected. Willie had his long-nosed automatic in hand. I had no doubt that he would use it if we were surprised by a guard.

As we approached the entrance from the side, Willie warned us again about making any noise. Then he kept us pressed against the wall while Z rounded the corner of the building. After a few minutes we heard a low whistle, and Willie shoved us ahead. A guard was standing stiffly before the door, his arms raised high. Z had his pistol trained on him. Willie rushed forward and removed the guard's weapons. Then, pulling two short lengths of rope and a gag from his pocket, he deftly wrapped up the guard like a Christmas present. All of this happened with incredible speed. Willie and Z were real professionals at their work.

Z peeled off his trench coat, revealing that he was wearing the same uniform as a plant guard. He entered the building, and Willie began to count backward from 20. ". . . 5, 4, 3, 2, 1. Now walk," he said, "and take it nice and easy."

We did as we were told. The lobby was empty, but another guard lay on the floor—out cold. A bump forming above his left ear testified to more of Z's professional work. Willie marched us along a corridor, then stopped before we reached a big glass window. Even from our angle we could see that it faced a room with computers and instruments—and controls.

By now I was past being scared. I felt numb, as if someone had hit me over the head. I tried to force myself to think. "Is he going to break the window?" I whispered to McGee.

He shook his head slightly. "It's half a foot thick."

Beyond the window was a door, which was under the surveillance of a television camera mounted on the ceiling. Z stood in front of it. In his hand was a key that he must have taken from the guard. He pressed a buzzer and immediately a voice answered over the intercom.

"Code?"

"It's Harper, sir. Sorry, but the police called. There's been an emergency at your home. I—"

A buzzer sounded back. Z had his key in the lock and the heavy steel door swung open. In an instant Z was inside. Propelled by Willie's knuckles in our backs, we were right behind him.

There were three men on duty in the control room—plant technicians dressed in khaki pants and shirts. They spun around at our abrupt entrance.

"What the . . ."

"Who are you?"

They didn't seem to believe what was happening. One moment the workings of this awesome plant had been in their hands; the next Z and Willie were in control.

Willie swung the door shut behind us and frisked the technicians; they were unarmed. Z forced them to lie on the floor, then shoved McGee and me up against one wall. Z must have been familiar with the plant, because in two or three quick motions he had pulled two levers and turned some knobs. Almost immediately a needle on one of the gauges started to rise. A red light flashed on the main console.

"What are you doing?" shouted one of the plant technicians, half on his feet. "You've turned off the cooling system and cut off the fail-safe!"

With a swift kick in the ribs Willie sent the technician reeling in pain.

"You fool! You'll cause a meltdown!" another man screamed.

Willie turned on him like an enraged beast and fired a shot just over his head. The bullet ricocheted wildly around the room.

"SILENCE!" shouted Z. "Next time Willie shoots to kill!"

The technicians cringed on the floor.

Then, in a softer voice, he said, "You're right, of course. Turning off the cooling system *will* cause a meltdown, and that's exactly what I'm ready to do: melt down the core and take a couple hundred thousand people with me. It will take just about two and a half hours."

One of the technicians began whimpering.

"You are insane," another dared to say. I thought Willie was going to kick him; instead he pointed his gun toward the observation window. A guard and a police officer were there. A second later they were at the door, the surveillance camera picking up their image and projecting it onto a screen inside the control room. A voice came over the intercom.

"This is the police. The plant is surrounded. Open the

door and come out with your hands up. If we have to break in, things will go much harder for you. Now open up!"

Z flicked the switch on the intercom and said, "By the time you break in, your technicians and these two kids will be dead. So you're not going to break in. Instead, you'll do exactly what I tell you to do. First get me the top man. I don't talk to flunkies." With that he flicked off the intercom.

We heard nothing further from outside, but I was sure that a SWAT team would be on the scene within minutes. I tried to think of what to do next, and I looked toward McGee. Even if he was as scared as me, I figured he would still think of something to do. Yet he just sat there, hunched over, staring at the floor. I wondered whether his ESP was working—whether he knew what was going to happen—but I was afraid to ask.

Now Z was bending over McGee. "What's the matter, kid?" he said, his voice filled with sarcasm. "Aren't you happy? You should be happy. I paid you a big compliment by inviting you to be with me instead of with the police while we took care of this little business. I didn't want you to be able to help them. No, you're going to use your telepathy to help *us*. All you have to do is let us know if the cops are pulling any- thing funny. If you don't, your friend here," Z poked the gun at my throat, "is going to die."

McGee said nothing, and Z kept talking. "Now I have a little job for you to help you pass the time. You're very smart and your father is a computer expert so you must know how to type computer instructions. I want you to sit at that console and type what I tell you to."

McGee didn't move. At a glance from Z, Willie walked over to McGee and kicked him hard in the hip. McGee winced and gave a cry. Another kick. McGee struggled to his feet and

sat at the console. It was then that I felt more helpless then I ever had in my life.

"Don't get any ideas," Z said in a silky voice. "This computer doesn't work any controls. It only gets data on what's happening and displays it on the screen. The data it presents is also visible to the officials and the police on the plant's closed-circuit TV. It will help them understand how bad things are getting." Z laughed and Willie echoed him.

Standing behind McGee, Z said, "Type the words *Current Status.*"

McGee typed out the words. Instantly the screen lit up and these words appeared:

CURRENT STATUS
DANGER: COOLING SYSTEM OFF
TIME TO MELTDOWN: 2 HOURS 15 MINUTES

Willie nudged my arm with his gun. "You know what that means, kid?"

I shook my head, but McGee said, "It means that in a little more than two hours, a complete meltdown can no longer be stopped. The radioactive core will melt through the concrete floor of the containment building and release a killing dose of radiation into the air."

"That's exactly right," Z said. "Willie, don't you wish you could be that smart?"

There were now half a dozen men on the other side of the observation window, some in plain clothes, some in uniform. We could see, looking at the surveillance camera, that the Chief of Police was standing by the door where he could use the intercom.

Z switched it on from our side. Speaking in a cool, even voice, he said, "We have turned off the cooling system. You can verify this by referring to your computer display screen. As you know, unless it is turned back on within two hours, a meltdown will be irreversible. That means you have until exactly 9:15 P.M. to turn the cooling system on. If you attempt to do so before we give you permission, then the three technicians and the two kids will die instantly. If you want to avoid harming them *and* prevent a nuclear catastrophe, you must do precisely what we tell you to do.

"At exactly 8:45 our associate will arrive in a car with the license plate GX-115. You will hand over to him ten million dollars in one-thousand-dollar bills. At 8:55 he will notify us, through you, by code that he has received these funds. You will allow us—and our hostages—to enter the car and leave through the main gate. Then you will be able to enter the control room and turn on the cooling system in time to prevent a meltdown.

"If you attempt to follow us or interfere with our escape, the hostages will be killed. If you do what we say, they will be released as soon as we are safely away. *Do not make any plan to thwart us.* If you do, ESP McGee will know about it through his psychic powers. We have ways of making him talk. And if the kid says you're planning to double cross us, we'll only surrender *after a meltdown is irreversible!* You can prevent a meltdown by paying us the money, or by sacrificing the hostages and breaking in. It's up to you."

A few minutes later, the Chief of Police replied: "We can't get ten million dollars that fast!"

"Of course you can," the terrorist leader snapped back. "None of the banks within a hundred miles will be worth a dime if this plant goes. Those bankers know how their bread is buttered—they'll get the money. Don't give us any more stories. Our demands are nonnegotiable!" Z snapped off the intercom.

The next half hour there was nothing to do but wait. We could see a couple policemen and officials looking on helplessly through the bullet-proof observation window. Other officers scurried around, setting up mobile phone equipment. I wondered what preparations they were making beyond our vision. The control room was so well fortified against unlawful intrusion, it would have been easy for the terrorists to kill us before the police could break in. But I imagined a SWAT team, like the one I'd seen on TV, waiting in the corridor, ready to dynamite the door and storm in with automatic weapons blazing. Or maybe they'd use nerve gas or something. I figured they'd probably called out the National Guard by now and even notified the President of the United States. And what were they broadcasting on TV and radio? Worst of all I thought how worried my family must be. I could almost see them in front of the TV—Mom sobbing a little and Dad trying to reassure her; Emily pale and wide-eyed, never turning from the TV set; Loser whining a little, sensing that something was wrong . . .

All the time these things were running through my

89

mind, I watched the electronic display screen, ticking off the minutes until meltdown. Suddenly a horn sounded a shrill blast and a second flashing red light came on. The screen said:

DANGER: COOLING SYSTEM OFF
TIME TO MELTDOWN: 1 HOUR 15 MINUTES

Z ignored the noise and kept staring at the screen, but Willie started pacing back and forth like a caged animal. "Stay in one place!" Z finally barked. Willie gave him a mean look, but he obeyed.

Then something happened that surprised me. McGee asked Z if he could request the computer to give a fuller status report. Z looked startled, but then he said, "Be my guest."

McGee typed in some instructions, but nothing happened. He couldn't seem to get the computer to give more information. Finally he gave up.

About half an hour later an electronic beeping tone began and the screen changed:

GRAVEST EMERGENCY: EVACUATE CITY
TIME TO MELTDOWN: 45 MINUTES

I looked over at Z. He was smiling! He thought that was just fine. McGee sat slumped over the console, looking forlorn. I had trouble fighting back the tears. McGee hadn't helped us. If anything, it seemed he had played into the terrorists' hands.

I waited. There was nothing else I could do. Everyone was tense. The technicians seemed to be suffering the most. One of them couldn't stop sobbing. Another was soaked through with sweat. The deadline was getting close. Suddenly the screen changed again:

NATIONAL ALERT: NOTIFY PRESIDENT
FULL EVACUATION SHOULD BE IN PROCESS
TIME TO MELTDOWN: 39 MINUTES

"They won't try to stall us now," Z said. "Ten million dollars, Willie. Think about it. The boss will treat us very well, very well indeed."

But Willie looked scared. He sat there passing his gun back and forth from one hand to the other. Suddenly he cried out, *"Suppose Gino doesn't show?"*

"Gino will show, Willie. Everything's been planned to the minute." Z sounded as if he were trying very hard to be patient.

I figured it was all over.

Then the red flashing light went off and a green light came on. Everyone fastened his eyes on the display screen. It said:

ALL CLEAR: CONDITIONS NORMAL
TIME TO MELTDOWN: 3 MINUTES

The terrorists were suddenly on their feet. "What's going on?" yelled Z.

"I don't know," cried McGee and one of the technicians at the same time.

The screen changed again.

ALL CLEAR: EMERGENCY CANCELED
TIME TO MELTDOWN: 2 MINUTES 55 SECONDS

Now the seconds were ticking off . . . 2:54 . . . 2:53 . . . 2:52 . . . and the screen was flashing:

EXIT!
EXIT!
EXIT!

"Two minutes!" Willie yelled, his eyes wild. "We've got to get out of here!" He started toward the door.

"Stop, you fool," Z screamed.

Willie unbolted the door and ran through. But Z didn't move. He seemed paralyzed.

"Dive," I yelled, and practically crashed into McGee as we both scampered under a desk. Out of the corner of my eye I saw a burly cop knock the gun out of Z's hand with a karate chop. Suddenly the control room was filled with the SWAT team, weapons trained everywhere. The technicians all had their hands in the air. Then McGee was yelling, "It's okay! It's okay!" The technicians rushed to the controls. We all waited anxiously for what seemed like forever, though it couldn't have been more than a minute; finally the screen flashed:

COOLING SYSTEM ON
ALL SYSTEMS RETURNING TO NORMAL

For the first time I thought to wipe the sweat off my forehead.

Chapter
Eleven

MCGEE walked calmly out of the building and I followed, thankful to be alive and free and out in the fresh air. The whole area in front of the plant was swarming with armed officers, police cars, fire engines, and TV film crew vans.

Then I saw the getaway car—a large station wagon with the license number GX-115. A man was facing it, his legs spread, his hands palm-down on the roof. One cop had a gun on him while two others frisked him from head to toe. The police chief hustled us past TV cameras and reporters and into a squad car.

"Your parents were mighty worried about you boys," the chief said. "They were ready to storm our road blocks to get through to the plant, but they agreed to wait at the Terrells' house as long as I promised to take you both there myself as soon as we got you out."

"We appreciate the ride," McGee said.

"We sure do," I said. But McGee and the chief had already started talking about the terrorists and police methods, and what the FBI was doing. I didn't want to interrupt, but I was dying of curiosity. And when we had almost reached my house, I finally broke in. "How did you do it, McGee?"

He sat sideways to face me and took a deep breath before replying. "It's like this. The display screen gives you the data you ask for. But it will also print any sequence of statements you give it at exactly the time you want them to appear on the screen. All I did was make it automatically print the words I knew would panic the terrorists—at thirty minutes before meltdown."

"But why did you make it say 'all clear' *and* '3 minutes to meltdown' at the same time?"

McGee smiled. "I wanted to scare them by making them think there were only three minutes left, so I set the countdown to start at three and print automatically, even though the *real* deadline didn't change. But if nothing else had appeared on the screen, they would have figured out that I was tricking them. That's why I had it print the opposite, 'all clear,' statement as well. The contradictory information confused them so much, they couldn't think things through. Willie's survival instinct took over and he ran; Z was so baffled he just froze."

I thought a moment about McGee's explanation and about Nina Ravinsky's opinions; then I said, "It sounds as if you weren't using ESP. You were using psychology and logic!"

"That explanation might be convincing, except that psychology is hardly an exact science and logic can be wrong-headed if you start from a false premise," McGee replied.

At that moment the car pulled up in front of our house. The chief gave just a touch of the siren to let my folks know we were there, and we'd hardly gotten out of the car when Mom and Dad and Emily came piling out of the door—Mr. and Mrs. McGee right behind them. Mr. McGee was holding his hands clasped over his head in a sort of victory salute. And my Dad yelled "Bravo" and Emily yelled "Whoopee!"

I sure felt good. We said good-bye to the police chief and thanked him and he thanked us. Mom asked him in but he said he had to go back to headquarters and wrap things up. Then we all went inside, where Mom had cider and donuts waiting.

Everyone was hugging and laughing and crying and talking at once when the doorbell rang. Dad opened the door and Loser came tearing into the house, jumping up and almost knocking me over. Then came Nina Ravinsky and her parents! I suddenly remembered that the last I'd seen of Loser, he'd been shut up in McGee's house.

Nina explained that she'd gone past the McGees' house around 6:45 P.M.—not long after we'd been taken prisoner—and she'd heard Loser howling.

"The door wasn't locked, so I opened it and there was Loser up at the top of the stairs. The cat—Harvey—had him trapped and he was afraid to come down, but I rescued him!" she said proudly. "Then I called the police. I knew something strange was going on."

"Thanks, Nina," I said, patting my heroic dog. "Loser, how could a big guy like you be afraid of a little cat?"

"You can't blame Loser," said Mr. McGee. "That cat is spooky."

"I agree," said Nina. "I hate to say it, Mrs. McGee, but when I was leading Loser out of the house, I noticed a lot of little fish bones on the hall rug."

Mrs. McGee looked pale, but it seemed to me that McGee had a little smile on his face. "We better be getting home," he said.

We all had another round of hugs, as if we were the survivors of a shipwreck and our lifeboat had just been rescued. As he was leaving, McGee thanked me for my help and said he hoped I'd be working with him in the future. "Though I think we deserve to sleep late tomorrow," he added with a smile.

"I'll go along with that," I grinned back.

The fact is, I'm already looking forward to our next case. Maybe I'll finally learn whether McGee has ESP.